The HUNCHBACK of NOTRE DAME

Acknowledgments

Artists Penko Gelev
Sotir Gelev

First edition for North America (including Canada and Mexico), Philippine Islands, and Puerto Rico published in 2007 by Barron's Educational Series, Inc.

All inquiries should be addressed to:
Barron's Educational Series, Inc.
250 Wireless Boulevard
Hauppauge, NY 11788
www.barronseduc.com

ISBN-13 (Hardcover): 978-0-7641-5979-4
ISBN-10 (Hardcover): 0-7641-5979-8
ISBN-13 (Paperback): 978-0-7641-3493-7
ISBN-10 (Paperback): 0-7641-3493-0

Library of Congress Control No.: 2005935392

Picture credits:
page 40 Alinari/TopFoto
page 41 Roger-Viollet/TopFoto
page 42 © The Salariya Book Company Ltd.
page 43 Digital Stock
page 44 RKO/The Kobal Collection
page 46 TopFoto/HIP
page 47 The Art Archive/Musée du Louvre Paris/Dagli Orti

Printed and bound in China
9 8 7 6 5 4 3 2 1

The HUNCHBACK of NOTRE DAME

VICTOR HUGO

illustrated by
Penko Gelev

BARRON'S

retold by
Michael Ford

series created and designed by
David Salariya

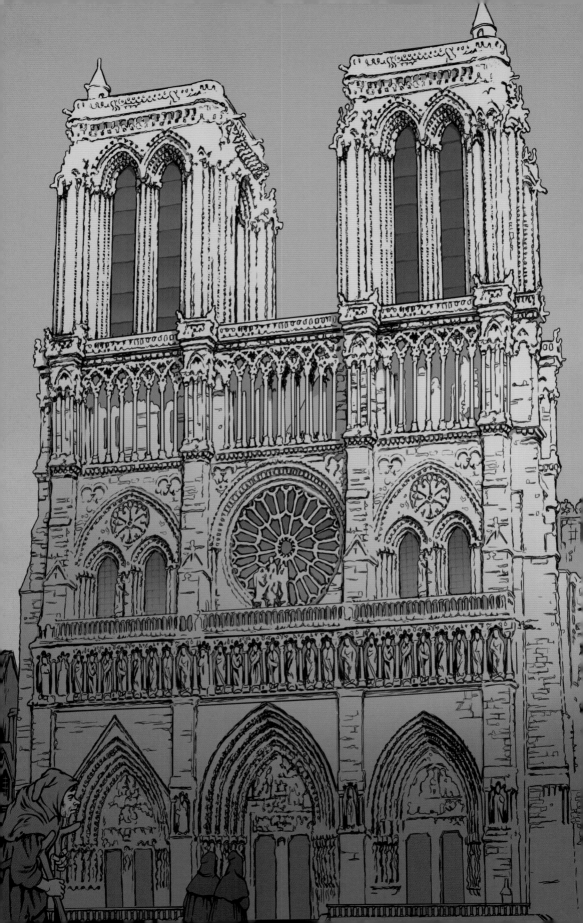

Three hundred and forty-eight years, six months, and nineteen days ago to-day, the Parisians awoke to the sound of all the bells in the triple circuit of the city, the university, and the town ringing a full peal.

Victor Hugo, The Hunchback of Notre Dame

CHARACTERS

Claude Frollo,
archdeacon of Notre Dame

Quasimodo,
hunchback

Pierre Gringoire,
playwright

Esmeralda,
Gypsy girl

Clopin Trouillefou,
beggar

Captain Phoebus de Chateaupers,
soldier

Fleur-de-Lys,
fiancée of Phoebus

Paquette,
old woman

PIERRE'S PLAY

January 6th, 1482

"The play! The play!"

In the Great Hall of the Palace of Justice in Paris, crowds have gathered to watch a play. Although the important guests are not yet there, the crowd is restless.

"Begin at once!"

Spectators bustle for space in the packed hall. A small group have even knocked out a window and sit high above, overlooking the stage. They shout for the play to start.

The actors are frightened of the mob. Although the Flemish ambassadors and royal guests haven't yet arrived, the play begins.[1]

"Charity, I beg you!"

However, the performance is soon interrupted. An old man in rags climbs onto the stage and shouts over the actors, begging for money.

"Begin again! Begin again!"

The man who wrote the play, Pierre Gringoire, is angry at the interruption. This is his chance for fame and fortune.

At that moment, the guests of honor arrive. They are here to celebrate the marriage of the King's son to Margaret of Flanders.[2] But they are late.

"Down with the play!"

The crowd is now noisy and unruly and have forgotten all about the play, Pierre Gringoire, and the old beggar, Clopin Trouillefou.[3]

1. Flemish: A person from Flanders (see below), it is also the language spoken there.
2. Flanders: A medieval state, now part of Belgium, the Netherlands, and France.
3. unruly: Difficult to control.

THE POPE OF FOOLS

I'll show you what we do in Flanders.

As the play cannot continue, one of the ambassadors suggests that the crowd instead has fun electing a "Pope of Fools" – the person who can make the ugliest face.

A small window is knocked out of the chapel opposite the Palace of Justice. This is where the contestants will appear.

Some of the crowd gather in the chapel, waiting unseen until it's their turn to display their ugliest faces. The contest begins right away.

One after another, the citizens of Paris make hideous faces through the window frame.

The crowd goes wild with excitement and laughter, as each person tries to outdo the last, until . . .

Oh, it's disgusting!

I've never seen anything like it!

Is that a mask?

. . . the crowd gasps. A face more repulsive than any other they have seen stares out from the chapel window.

It's Quasimodo!

The bristly hair, the huge swollen eye, the misshaped skull – the mob have a clear winner. Someone recognizes the face as that of Quasimodo, the bell ringer of Notre Dame cathedral.

The people call for Quasimodo to come out and receive his "prize." They clap and cheer until the deaf hunchback appears.

A young man emerges from the crowd and points at Quasimodo's face. He teases the poor wretch, laughing at his deformity and ugliness.

However, the man gets more than he bargained for. With great strength, Quasimodo strikes him in the chest and sends him flying backwards, limbs flailing.

The crowd laughs and applauds the spectacle. They then dress Quasimodo in a robe like the Pope and crown him with a jester's hat.

Quasimodo is not used to so much attention. He smiles happily as several strong men place him on a throne and carry him aloft for all the city to see.

Pierre Gringoire watches in dismay. He cannot understand why the people would rather watch Quasimodo than his masterpiece. What an ignorant mob!

9

ESMERALDA

"What a fine mob of fools Parisians are!"

With the procession out of sight, Pierre walks the streets feeling sorry for himself. His chance of fame is over, his hopes of riches gone.

Suddenly he hears a cry of "Esmeralda! Esmeralda!" from the nearby Place de Grève. He runs around the corner and sees a Gypsy girl dancing.

Her face is lit by the bonfire that blazes in the square. Her hair is as dark as a raven's feathers. Her eyes, too, are almost as black.

A crowd looks on in silence, enchanted by the sight of the beautiful young woman dancing before them. She is known as Esmeralda.

I think I'm in love.

Pierre is enchanted, too. He forgets all about his failed play and watches her as well.

Esmeralda is not dancing alone. She is accompanied by a white goat, which seems to understand her commands and performs tricks.

Come Djali, dance!

The crowd clap and throw money to the girl and her amazing pet goat. She then begins to sing.

Esmeralda's beautiful voice rings out clearly, until she is interrupted by the shouts of an old woman from the nearby Tower of Roland.

Will you be quiet, you cricket from hell!

The devil take the old hag!

The crowd is angry and hurls abuse at the elderly woman, whose name is Paquette, telling her to put an end to her curses.

Just then, the "Pope of Fools" procession bursts onto the square, carrying Quasimodo. All the thieves, ruffians, and beggars of the city have joined them.

At that moment, a hand reaches out and pulls the hunchback from his seat, tearing off his cloak. It is the archdeacon of Notre Dame, Claude Frollo.[1] The crowd look on in terror – will the great fists crush the man of God?

But oddly it's Quasimodo who looks afraid.

The two men do not speak to each other. Instead, they communicate using a sort of sign language, making shapes with their hands that no one else can understand.

Much to the crowd's surprise and disappointment, the archdeacon leads Quasimodo away in the direction of the cathedral.

1. archdeacon: A senior minister in the Christian church.

QUASIMODO'S UPBRINGING

Sixteen years before . . .

Morning mass has just finished in Notre Dame cathedral. People are filing out of the great doors ready to go home.

Sister, whatever can that be?

Inside, four old ladies are gathered around the foundlings' bed. This is where unwanted babies are left by mothers who cannot care for them.

It's a deformed ape!

Inside the crib is a strange, ugly baby, crying out loudly. It has bristly hair and its face is twisted out of shape. None of the women want to care for the poor child.

I'll adopt that child.

However, a young priest called Claude Frollo approaches. He feels sorry for the unusual child and decides to bring him up as if he were his own.

Wrapping the baby in the folds of his gown, he carries him away. He names the little one Quasimodo, meaning "almost."

As the boy grows older, Claude looks after him as a father, showing him the cloisters, chapels and corridors of the huge cathedral where he lives.

In time, young Quasimodo learns the secrets of Notre Dame better than anyone. He rarely leaves the confines of its cold stone walls.

When the boy hunchback does venture outside, it is never a happy experience. Children throw stones and chase him with barking dogs.

Each time the priest and his adopted son leave the cathedral together, people whisper and point at the odd pair.

Due to his harsh treatment, Quasimodo learns to have respect for only one man – his savior, father, and only friend, Claude Frollo.

When Quasimodo is older, Claude gives his son a job. He must climb the many stairs to the top of Notre Dame's bell tower . . .

. . . and ring the great cathedral bells.

There is nothing the hunchback loves more dearly than making the bells swing with all his strength and feeling them shudder as they make their wonderful sound.

But, you may ask, how he can stand the crashing and booming of the bells so high in the tower? Well, dear reader, it is because over the years, that very noise has made him deaf!

KIDNAP AND RESCUE

Back in 1482 . . .

Is someone following me?

The crowds from the Fool's parade have gone home to bed. It is a cold night and Esmeralda is making her way home with Djali.

She is being followed by Pierre Gringoire. He is curious to see where she lives. Hearing a noise behind her, Esmeralda peers back into the darkness.

All she can see are shadows in the dim streets. She turns quickly into a side road.

Suddenly, Pierre hears a scream from the alley into which she has stepped. He runs after her, no longer worried about being seen.

Help! Help me!

What's this?

Pierre sees two men struggling with Esmeralda. One is the hunchback who lives in Notre Dame. The other wears a hooded cloak.

Before Pierre can do anything, Quasimodo steps forward and swings his great arm at him. The blow sends Pierre flying.

Murder! Murder!

Pierre sees the hunchback pick up the Gypsy girl as though she weigh nothing and set off down the alleyway with her.

Help me!

But Quasimodo does not get far. Blocking his path is a soldier on horseback. Confused, the hunchback halts and the soldier seizes the girl from him.

Quasimodo rushes forward, trying to grab the girl from the soldier on horseback, but is immediately surrounded by more heavily armed soldiers.

Quasimodo was seized and, although he struggled violently, the soldiers overpowered him and he was soon bound tightly by rope.

The Gypsy and the soldier stare deeply into each other's eyes. The man introduces himself as Captain Phoebus de Chateaupers.

Esmeralda blushes and thanks the captain, before sliding from the saddle and disappearing into the night.

THE KINGDOM OF TRUANDS

The mud of Paris is especially stinking!

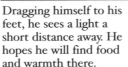

Sir, sir, a piece of bread?

Pierre's day is going from bad to worse. He lies bruised and freezing in a stinking gutter.

Dragging himself to his feet, he sees a light a short distance away. He hopes he will find food and warmth there.

As he approaches, he finds the path littered with beggars, vagrants, and cripples begging for money. He tries to ignore them and continue to where the light is coming from . . . but it seems they have other ideas.

Catch him!

As he pushes past, they start to chase after him, throwing aside their crutches and sticks! Pierre is herded into a large hall filled with beggars and cripples where a large fire blazes – the infamous Court of Miracles!

Welcome to my court.

What is it to be?

Pierre finds himself in front of a man seated on a barrel. It is none other than the beggar who interrupted his play – Clopin Trouillefou! All around the hall, the city's lowlifes are drinking, dancing, and making merry.

Here the old man is not a beggar, but a king – the King of Truands![1] Clopin tells Pierre that he must pay a fine for entering his kingdom uninvited, or be hanged!

1. truands: An old French word meaning vagabond or beggar.

When Pierre says that he doesn't have a single coin upon him, Clopin tells him that there is only one way to save his life – to join their gang . . . but first he must pass a test.

They hang up a gown covered in bells. Pierre must climb a stool, reach into the pocket, and take a purse from it without making the bells sound.

He fails miserably. The crowd goes wild with excitement, and poor Pierre is pale with fear as the "executioner" fixes a noose around his neck.

However, King Clopin offers him a final chance to be saved. It is a truand custom, he says, that a man can be spared from hanging if someone in the room agrees to marry him.

Things are not looking good for Pierre until, at the last minute, the crowd parts and Esmeralda steps forward. She is willing to be wed to the condemned man – he is saved!

QUASIMODO AT THE PILLORY

The next day, at the Place de Grève, a huge crowd has gathered. Word has it that a public flogging will take place, and there are few things the bloodthirsty people of Paris enjoy more.

It's the bell ringer!

A cart rumbles into the square. On it, bound tightly with ropes and chains, is poor Quasimodo. He does not struggle as he is led toward the central pillory.[1]

Nor does he make a sound when soldiers strip him to the waist and fasten him securely to the wheel in front of the crowd.

A man steps up to the platform carrying a long whip of knotted leather. He rolls up his sleeves and flexes his muscles.

An hourglass filled with sand is turned over, indicating that the performance will begin.

The wheel begins to turn, but the hunchback does not yet understand. As the first lash cuts into his back, Quasimodo's eye opens with pain.

Lash him harder!

The flogging gets harder and harder until blood pours down the poor hunchback's sides. The crowd howls and laughs, taunting Quasimodo. Stones and rotting food are thrown at him, too.

1. pillory: A wooden stage or frame on which criminals were tied to suffer public abuse and ridicule.

You ugly wretch!

Quasimodo struggles with his bonds but cannot escape. The mob cheers to see him struggle and fail. Though he cannot hear them, Quasimodo sees the hate on their faces.

Suddenly he stops struggling. Something has caught his eye, and he stares across the heads of the jeering crowd.

It is Claude Frollo, his adoptive father and master! He must have come to put an end to his son's terrible suffering. Quasimodo is relieved to see him.

But, after looking on for a few moments, the archdeacon urges his horse to walk on. Turning his back on Quasimodo, he abandons him to the crowd.

The light of hope in Quasimodo's eye disappears. He cries out in pain, and begs the crowd for a drink of water.

Water! Please! Water!

Esmeralda steps forward and holds a flask to the hunchback's mouth. The crowd goes silent. In gratitude, he tries to kiss the Gypsy's hand. But the girl pulls away, frightened.

Curses on you, daughter of Egypt!

Suddenly, from the barred window of a cell nearby, a terrible screech is heard. Curses aimed at the Gypsy pierce the silence.

THE TRAGIC TALE OF PAQUETTE

The voice from the cell in the Tower of Roland belongs to Paquette. She had once been an attractive young girl.

After her parents died, Paquette had given birth to a beautiful baby daughter. She christened the child Agnes, meaning "lamb."

Paquette doted on her baby, the only love in her life, and dressed her up as finely as a princess, even though she herself was poor.

She even made little Agnes a pair of pink boots from the finest silk. Paquette loved to kiss the child's tiny feet and toes.

But her happiness would soon end. When the child was about one year old, a group of travelling Gypsies came to the town where Paquette and Agnes lived.

Can you tell me the way to . . .

They were petty thieves and fortune tellers who used tricks to make a living in the area. Soon, all the local people came to fear and avoid them.

Where is my Agnes?

One day, Paquette briefly left the house to see a friend. When she returned, little Agnes's cot was empty. Her child was missing – Agnes had been stolen!

Where is my only treasure?

The only sign left of Agnes was a single pink boot. Paquette was terrified. Who could take a defenseless baby from its mother?

Agnes! Has anyone seen my child?

Waaa! Waaa!

Paquette ran in panic through the streets, crying out for her poor child.

When she finally returned home, neighbors told her they had seen Gypsies creeping into her house with a bundle of rags. Hearing a child crying inside, Paquette was overjoyed.

No!

What have they done with Agnes?

But when she burst in, she got a nasty surprise. Instead of her beautiful Agnes, the baby in the cot looked more like a pig than a human.

Paquette rushed to where the Gypsies were camped outside the town, but found only the embers of a fire and some of Agnes's torn clothes. They had gone!

My little girl has gone forever!

The distraught mother thought that the Gypsies had eaten her baby.[1] She cried for months, clutching all that remained of her lost daughter, her tiny pink boot.

Eventually, unable to continue with life, Paquette locked herself in the Rat Hole, by the Place de Grève, vowing never to come out again.[2]

You, reader, now know what became of the deformed child. He was taken to Notre Dame and adopted by a priest.

1. distraught: Very upset.
2. the Rat Hole: Another name for the Tower of Roland, where Paquette shut herself away.

A JEALOUS RAGE

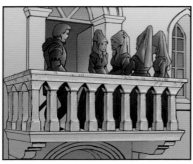

It is several weeks since the truand "marriage" of Pierre and Esmeralda. Opposite Notre Dame, on the balcony of a mansion, stand Captain Phoebus and his fiancée, Fleur-de-Lys.

The Captain is bored with Fleur-de-Lys and her friends. Looking over the balcony, he sees Esmeralda dancing below.

What a sight!

He is not the only one watching her. From the walls of Notre Dame, Claude Frollo is staring at Esmeralda with a strange look in his eyes.

Little one! Come hither.

Fleur-de-Lys sees the girl too. She calls for Esmeralda to come to their rooms to perform for them.

When Esmeralda climbs the stairs and enters, Phoebus is struck once again by her enchanting beauty. He can hardly take his eyes from her.

Esmeralda can see the desire in the captain's eyes. Believe it or not, dear reader, she fell in love with him at first sight. But she is ashamed to show her feelings in front of Phoebus's fiancée.

Esmeralda turns and runs from the room. Fleur-de-Lys is angry as she watches her fiancé follow the beautiful Gypsy girl out onto the street below.

I must see you later!

When Phoebus catches up with Esmeralda, he whispers that he would like to meet her later that evening. She agrees.

Later that evening, Captain Phoebus waits for Esmeralda as agreed. However, he is not alone – a sinister hooded figure watches from the shadows.

I will wait for them in here.

When the figure sees that the couple is about to go inside, he sneaks into the building ahead of them. He hides himself carefully in a cupboard and waits for them to enter.

Phoebus leads Esmeralda inside. They are about to kiss, when suddenly the cupboard bursts open. It is Archdeacon Frollo, holding a knife!

Aaargh!

He plunges the blade into the captain's back. Phoebus cries out in surprise and pain. Esmeralda screams.

The couple collapses to the floor. Phoebus is unconscious, and the Gypsy girl has fainted. Suddenly, Frollo hears footsteps approaching, attracted by the screams and sounds of a struggle.

Seeing no other way to escape, Frollo quickly leaps from the window into the cold waters of the River Seine below.

THE TRIAL OF ESMERALDA

What has happened here?

Esmeralda wakes as she hears the sound of boots thundering up the stairs. But she is trapped beneath Pheobus's body!

Soldiers storm into the room. What do they see? Their captain, with a bloody knife sticking out of his back, and there with him, the Gypsy girl.

Esmeralda is arrested, accused of being a murderer and a witch. Even Djali the goat does not escape; they say he is the devil in disguise.

I saw everything.

At the Palace of Justice, the court of judges comes together for Esmeralda's trial. She shakes with fear as the old men in the council of judges stare down at her.

A witness says that she saw Esmeralda enter the building with Captain Phoebus, who looked as though he were under a spell.

That goat must have transformed into a phantom priest!

The old woman then heard a scream from the bedroom, but when she entered, all she saw was a black-robed figure fly out of the window.

The judges talk together before casting their verdict: guilty of witchcraft and murder! This means she will be sent to the gallows![1] They turn to Esmeralda. Will she admit her guilt, or die unrepentant?[2]

1. gallows: A wooden frame where executed criminals were hung for public viewing.
2. unrepentant: Showing no regret.

I deny everything!

Do not struggle.

Esmeralda denies the charges; she is innocent! But this angers the judges! She is taken down to the dungeon to be tortured.

No, I am innocent.

I confess! Have mercy!

As the torturer fits a buskin to her leg, he asks her once more to admit she is a witch.[1] Bravely, innocent Esmeralda refuses.

As the screws are turned, the contraption cruelly squeezes the girl's leg. The pain is worse than she ever imagined. She screams in pain and terror.

The blade entered deep.

Leave me, you monster!

Having confessed her guilt, Esmeralda is thrown into a cold, damp cell to await her terrible fate. She is to be hung from the gallows in the Place du Grève.

While there, she has an unexpected and unwelcome visitor – the wicked archdeacon. He taunts her through the bars of her cell, describing how he stabbed Phoebus, and telling her that the handsome captain is dead.

1. buskin: An instrument of torture covering the foot and/or the lower part of the leg.

SANCTUARY!

But Captain Phoebus is not dead. He has recovered from his wound and is going about his business as usual.

Where have you been?

I was merely wounded, a mere scratch.

Several days later, Phoebus visits his fiancée once again. She wants to know where he has been, so he tells her that he was injured in the line of duty.

Bring out the devil's servant!

Below her apartment, huge crowds have gathered to witness the execution of Esmeralda, the Gypsy girl to be hung as a witch.

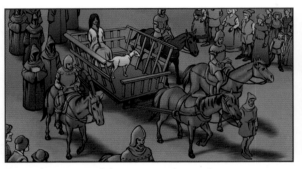

From the corner of the square, a horse-drawn cart appears. In the cart are Esmeralda and her pet goat, Djali. A noose is already knotted around the poor girl's slender neck.

Tears run down Esmeralda's face. She is crying, not just for herself and Djali, but because she believes her beloved Phoebus is dead. Can anything save her?

She will be confessed.

She gets down from the cart in front of the huge doors of Notre Dame. A procession of priests slowly descends the steps, led by Archdeacon Claude Frollo.

Be mine and I will help you!

Everybody thinks he has come to bless the prisoner. But when he gets close, he whispers that her life can be saved if she promises to love him.

"Be gone, Satan!"

Esmeralda despises him more than anyone in the world and refuses his offer. Laughing, he withdraws into the cathedral.

No one has noticed, but high above, the hunchback has been watching from the cathedral walls. He cannot watch the beautiful Gypsy girl perish.

As she is led to be hung, the crowd hears a mighty roar from the skies above.

"Sanctuary! Sanctuary!¹"

The crowd points and stares as Quasimodo swings down from the masonry on a rope. He pushes away the guards who are holding Esmeralda as though they were made of paper. The crowd is astonished.

Quasimodo scoops up the terrified girl and hurries into the cathedral. He knows that she will be protected within the walls of this house of God. She has sanctuary and is safe . . . for now.

1. sanctuary: Medieval law stated that once inside a church, a person was safe from arrest.

A FRIENDSHIP GROWS

Claude Frollo is unaware of this dramatic rescue. He laughs to himself, thinking Esmeralda is dead.

Later that night, he is walking through the galleries of Notre Dame. But what is this? The ghost of Esmeralda has come to haunt him! Terrified, the archdeacon flees.

But, of course, Esmeralda is not a ghost. Quasimodo has found her a small room, safely hidden away high up in the cathedral.

The hunchback tries to comfort her, bringing blankets to keep her warm and food and drink so that she will not go hungry. However, she is still scared of him.

No matter what he does for her, she is still too frightened to look at him. Her terrible fear makes him feel sad and lonely.

Poor Quasimodo understands that he is ugly and that the Gypsy girl can never love him. He promises to stay out of her way as much as possible.

He gives Esmeralda a special whistle. Though he is unable to hear people's voices, he can hear the high-pitched noise of the whistle.

Now you will be mine!

Later that night, while Esmeralda sleeps, a figure approaches in the darkness. It is Archdeacon Frollo. He has silently come in to take Esmeralda away.

When she wakes and sees Frollo's cruel face above her, Esmeralda gasps in terror. He tries to grab her, but she struggles free.

Help, a vampire!

She manages to put the whistle to her lips. Quasimodo hears its sound, even on the other side of the cathedral.

Quasimodo bursts into the room and pulls the attacker away by the throat. He is about to snap the wretch's neck in two, when he sees whose face he is holding.

I cannot...

No one shall have her then!

Quasimodo's anger turns to confusion. He cannot bring himself to kill the man who has been a father to him. The evil priest scurries away like a beetle as soon as he is released.

29

THE CATHEDRAL UNDER ATTACK

"I have a plan."

Claude Frollo needs to find a way past Esmeralda's guardian. He arranges to meet Pierre Gringoire, her husband.

"She saved your life. Now you must save hers."

The archdeacon tells Pierre that the authorities are planning to arrest Esmeralda whether she is inside the cathedral or not.

"Think of the gold!"

There isn't much time, so Pierre organizes the community of truands. Their plan is to storm the cathedral and rescue Esmeralda themselves, stealing the church's gold and treasures as well.

The ragged band approach the cathedral. The men are armed with whatever they could lay their hands on, bars, mallets, and pitchforks.

"Follow me! Sack the cathedral![1]"

Clopin Troufillou, dressed in his best rags, leads the beggar army. At his signal, they charge forward and attack Notre Dame.

A small group rush at the doors with their weapons and set about trying to break in, hammering on the wood. However, they don't get very far.

"Aaaaargh!"

A huge wooden beam crashes down from above, crushing several men. Screams of pain come from the injured. Where did the beam come from? The heavens?

"To the doors, comrades!"

However, Clopin is not deterred. He organizes several more men and they pick up the heavy beam to use as a battering ram. They charge at the doors.

30   1. sack: To rob and destroy something like a building or a city.

But they had not counted on the determination of Quasimodo. From high above, he hurls pieces of masonry at the attackers.

Men shout and flee as the boulders shower down upon them, killing and maiming many. But soon the hunchback runs out of stones to throw at them.

Quasimodo still has one more trick up his sleeve though. Over a fire, he melts lead sheets from the cathedral roof. He then pours the scalding molten metal onto the invaders.

Realizing they cannot enter the cathedral while the hunchback is guarding the doorway, the beggar's army changes its tactics.

Henceforth they'll call you "the blind one."

They scale ladders to get closer to Quasimodo. One fires a crossbow, aiming for the hunchback's eye, but the arrow misses its target.

Quasimodo does not even flinch as he snaps off the arrow's shaft. Now his attackers really begin to worry – there are no more arrows left!

With a mighty push, Quasimodo topples the ladders, sending the men to their deaths on the hard pavement of the square below.

A Noble Choice

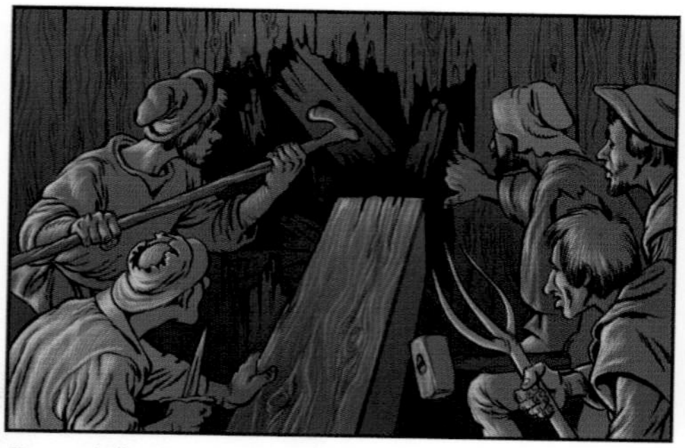

But while Quasimodo has been distracted, the truands have broken through the cathedral doors. They are about to enter, when they hear the sound of approaching hooves.

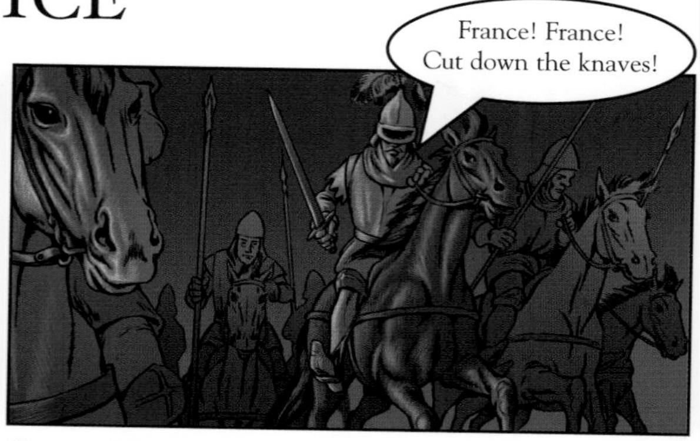
France! France! Cut down the knaves!

Captain Phoebus and the city's soldiers have come to put an end to the raid on Notre Dame. They gallop into the square, brandishing their swords and spears.

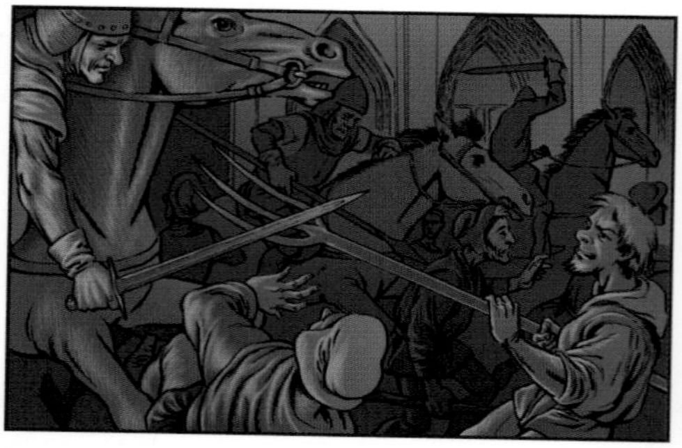

The ill-equipped truands are no match for armed soldiers on horseback. They fight bravely, but are defeated. Even "King" Clopin is killed by musket fire.

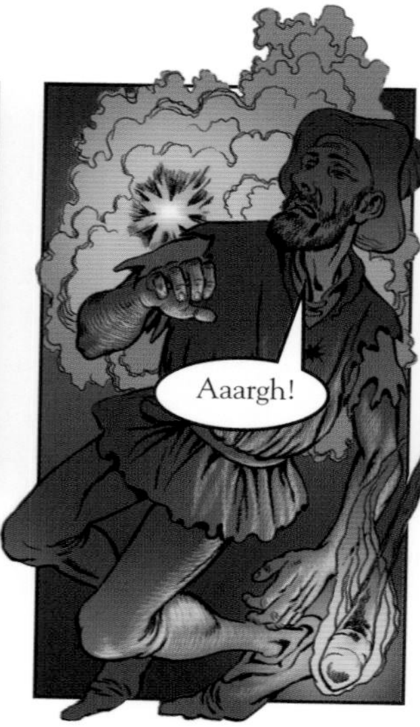
Aaargh!

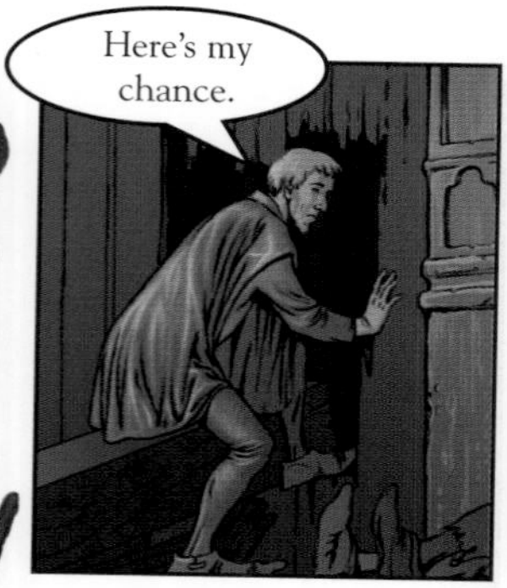
Here's my chance.

Amid the confusion, one person enters the cathedral – it is Pierre Gringoire. He has another plan to rescue Esmeralda.

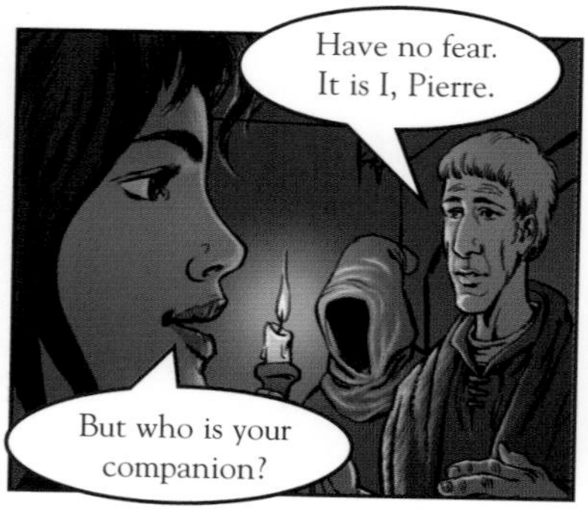
Have no fear. It is I, Pierre.
But who is your companion?

Esmeralda is pleased to see Pierre, but is suspicious of the mysterious cloaked figure with him.

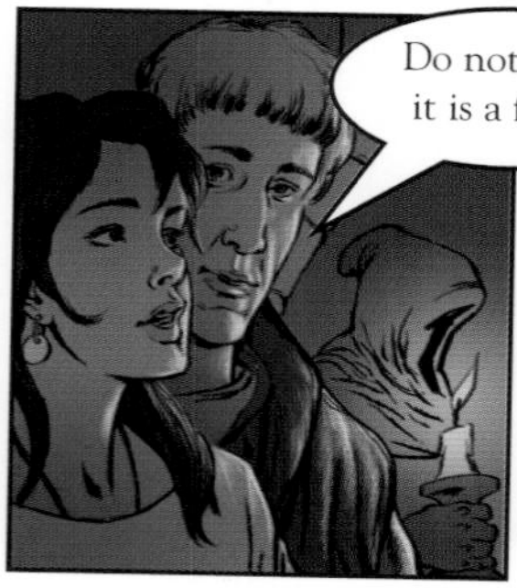
Do not worry, it is a friend.

Pierre reassures her that they have both come to take her to safety.

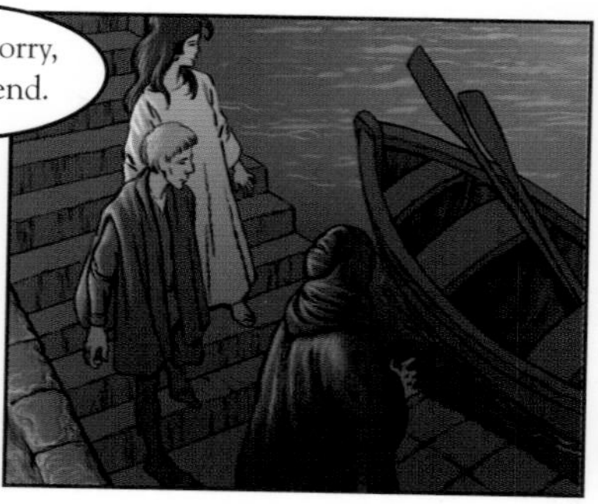

The three fugitives flee through a secret door at the back of the cathedral. There is a small boat waiting for them on the river.

Find the Gypsy woman! Death to her!

Once aboard, the hooded companion rows silently across the dark waters of the River Seine. They have escaped! Or have they?

On the far bank, they look back at the cathedral, dark against the night sky. Suddenly they hear soldiers. Frightened, Pierre dashes away without a word.

I knew it was you again.

I love you! It is true, I do!

It is Phoebus whom I love, murderer!

The stranger pulls back his hood – it is Archdeacon Frollo! Esmeralda lets out a gasp. They are alone in the Place de Grève.

Before Esmeralda can flee, he begs her to run away with him. He says he has always loved her, that she has enchanted him.

He tries to kiss her, but she can think of nothing worse than kissing this evil man who killed her beloved Phoebus. She struggles desperately to push him away.

I have you now!

Don't let her go.

Suddenly a pair of hands shoots out through the bars of a window behind them, seizing Esmeralda. It is Paquette, the old woman who hates all Gypsies.

Paquette grips Esmeralda tightly. Archdeacon Frollo tells her to hold the girl while he fetches soldiers to arrest her. If he cannot have her, no one will.

MOTHER AND DAUGHTER

Paquette lets out a terrible laugh and gleefully tells Esmeralda that she will soon be dead. She will finally have her revenge on Gypsies for killing her little Agnes.

Esmeralda is terrified. She does not know why the old hag hates her so much. She pleads for Paquette to free her.

In a whisper, Paquette tells Esmeralda all about her daughter who was taken by Gypsies, and how her own life was filled with sadness.

Esmeralda begs for mercy. She tells Paquette that she too has suffered. She lost her parents when she was so young that she cannot even remember them.

Paquette pulls out the only thing she has that belonged to her little Agnes. It is one of the pretty pink boots that her daughter wore.

Trembling, Esmeralda pulls out a matching pink boot tied around her own neck. Paquette's eyes open wide in surprise. Can it be true?

Recognition dawns on both their faces. Esmeralda is the child Paquette thought lost forever, and Paquette is the mother whom Esmeralda could not recall. They embrace, with tears of joy running down their faces.

At that moment, soldiers burst into the square. They roughly seize the Gypsy girl and tear her from the arms of her newfound mother.

Mother and daughter are both crying. The soldiers drag Paquette out of her cell, but she clings frantically to Esmeralda with a vicelike grip.

The scene before them is so touching it melts the soldiers' hearts. They let mother and daughter share one final embrace, but they have orders to carry out.

Tearing mother and daughter apart, the soldiers carry Esmeralda off to her terrible fate. Paquette watches helplessly.

Unable to cope with her grief, the old woman falls to the floor and doesn't stir. Paquette could not stand to lose her daughter again, and dies from a broken heart.

THE DEATH OF ESMERALDA

In Notre Dame, Quasimodo cannot find Esmeralda. He hurries through the cathedral in a panic, searching for her.

He sees Archdeacon Frollo wandering through the cathedral. He has a triumphant look in his eyes that makes Quasimodo suspicious.

The hunchback follows him to an upper balcony of the cathedral, where he stares out at the Place de Grève in the distance.

Quasimodo follows the direction of the priest's gaze, and sees a figure in white being carried up to the gallows.

Quasimodo gasps in horror! He thinks he recognizes the figure far below.

The noose is tied to the gallows and the ladder is kicked away. As the truth dawns, Quasimodo's heart almost stops: it is Esmeralda!

As the rope around her neck tightens, Archdeacon Frollo lets out a terrible, evil cackle of delight. His curse has gone forever.

In a fury, Quasimodo rushes forward and does what he should have done long before now. He pushes the cruel priest over the balcony edge.

Frollo hangs desperately to one of the stone gargoyles.[1] Below in the square, people hear the noises and look up.

But Quasimodo does not even look at the archdeacon. He is staring into the square, tears rolling down his deformed face.

Finally, the priest falls. He spins through the air, his robes flapping in the wind. He lets out a scream.

As he plummets to earth, his fall is broken by a rooftop. He struggles to stop himself slipping further but is too weak to hang on.

With a sickening thud he hits the cobbles below. Crowds gather around the crumpled, broken body: Archdeacon Frollo is dead.

1. gargoyle: Frightening stone carvings often seen on medieval churches that carry rainwater away from the walls.

Two Marriages

So, how does this tragic story end? Well, the coward Pierre Gringoire did at least manage to save Djali, the goat. He even becomes a successful writer of tragedies!

Captain Phoebus, for all his unfaithfulness, gets what he well and truly deserves. He marries the dull Fleur-de-Lys but is never truly happy, as his heart can never forget the beautiful Gypsy girl, Esmeralda.

In his sorrow, Quasimodo disappears from Notre Dame, leaving the great bells silent. No one in Paris knows his whereabouts.

The dead body of poor Esmeralda is taken from the gallows to a tomb at Montfaucon, where others like her are buried.[1] Here she will rest in peace.

1. Montfaucon: This was the site of the gallows in medieval Paris.

Look here.

But that is not quite the end of the tale. This, after all, is a love story, albeit a sad one. Many years later, two men were searching the great vault beneath Montfaucon.

What they discovered there, among the gloom, cobwebs, and skeletons, will live on forever in legend.

When the explorers tried to part the two skeletons, the larger of the two disintegrated to dust at their touch. They were obviously meant to be together forever.

They found two skeletons wrapped in a curious embrace. One was small, almost childlike, possibly that of a young woman, clutching a child's boot; the other was much larger, with an oddly misshapen spine.

Well, dear reader, we know that the skeletons were those of Quasimodo and Esmeralda. The hunchback was finally able to be with the Gypsy girl he loved so dearly, but only in death.

The End

VICTOR HUGO (1802 – 1885)

Victor-Marie Hugo was born in Besançon in France on February 26, 1802. He was the son of Joseph-Léopold-Sigisbert Hugo and Sophie Trébuchet. Hugo's father was an officer in Napoleon's army who loved danger and adventure. Their marriage was not a happy one; both were unfaithful but stayed together nonetheless. In 1807, Sophie moved the family from Paris to Italy for two years, while Léopold served as governor of a province near Naples. When he later moved to Spain, Sophie again joined him. It is thought that Sophie's lover was General Victor Lahorie, who was shot by a firing squad for plotting against Napoleon.

Portrait of Victor Hugo.

EDUCATION AND EARLY CAREER

From 1815 to 1818 Victor attended school in Paris. He began to write at a young age, and seemed drawn to poetry. He also translated the ancient Roman poet Virgil. Victor wanted to make a name for himself and be remembered after he was dead. As a boy he wrote:

"Many a great poet is often
Nothing but a literary giraffe:
How great he seems in front,
How small he is behind!"

Victor published his first collection of poems in 1822. King Louis XVIII was so impressed that he gave him a royal pension (a gift of money). Victor made his debut as a novelist with *Han d'Islande* in 1823, which was initially published anonymously.

MARRIAGE

In 1822, a year after his mother's death, Hugo married Adèle Foucher, the daughter of an officer at the French War Ministry. Unfortunately, Victor's brother Eugéne was secretly in love with Adèle and, after going mad on their wedding day, spent the rest of his life in an asylum. Adèle herself later published a biography of her husband.

A LIFE IN LITERATURE

Victor wrote a great deal during his life: novels, plays, poetry, and essays. He was an important figure in French literature and, along with *Notre Dame de Paris*, his other most famous work is undoubtedly *Les Misérables*, an epic story about social injustice.

In the 1830s Victor published several volumes of poetry, which were inspired by Juliette Drouet. She was an actress with whom Victor was romantically involved until her death in 1882.

In his forties, Victor became a member of the Académie Française, an exclusive group of intellectuals who discussed important matters of literature. However in the midst of triumph, tragedy awaited. In 1843, Victor's daughter, Léopoldine and her new husband drowned. In Hugo's poem, *Tomorrow, at Daybreak*, he describes visiting her grave:

"I shall not look on the gold of evening falling
Nor on the sails descending distant towards Harfleur,
And when I come, shall lay upon your grave
A bouquet of green holly and of flowering briar."

POLITICAL EXILE

Victor dedicated himself to politics as much as literature, supporting the Republican form of government. However, when Napoleon III claimed power in France in 1851, Victor believed his life was in danger. He fled the country, first to Brussels and then to Jersey in the Channel Islands. When he was later expelled from there, he moved with his family to Guernsey, another island in the English Channel.

Although in 1859 Napoleon III granted an amnesty to all political exiles (he said they could return to Paris with no fear of punishment), Victor was suspicious and chose not to return. Political troubles continued in France until 1870 when Napoleon III was overthrown and the "Third Republic" proclaimed. It was now safe for Victor to come home.

FINAL YEARS AND DEATH

Victor Hugo suffered a mild stroke in June 1878 but survived. He died in Paris on May 22, 1885 at age 83. He was given a national funeral, which more than two million people attended. He was buried in the Panthéon, a special building where only the greatest of France's citizens are entombed. Other famous French figures buried there include Marie Curie, Louis Braille, and Emile Zola.

Victor Hugo's funeral procession makes its way through Paris to the Panthéon, 1885.

Biography of Notre Dame

Some parts of the cathedral of Notre Dame have been standing for over 800 years. Much of the building has not changed since the period in which Victor Hugo's novel is set, at the end of the 15th century. Here is a brief timeline telling how the cathedral was built.

1160
Maurice de Sully, the Bishop of Paris, announces his plans to build a cathedral.

1163
Cornerstone laid, construction begins.

1182
Apse and choir completed.

1185
Heraclius calls for the Third Crusade from Notre Dame.

1196
Death of Maurice de Sully, nave completed.

1200
Work begins on the western façade.

1225
Western façade and rose window completed.

1250
Western towers and northern rose window completed.

1250 – 1300
Remaining elements completed.

1338 – 1453
The Hundred Years War between France and England.

1431
Henry VI of England crowned King of France within Notre Dame.

1548
Huguenots critical of the Catholic Church damage some features of the cathedral following the Council of Trent.

1558
The Dauphin Francois weds Mary Stuart (Mary I of Scotland) at Notre Dame.

1572
Henry of Navarre (later Henry IV of France) weds Marguerite of Valois.

1699
Reconstruction of main altar begins.

1741
Stained glass windows removed.

1793
Revolutionaries vandalize Notre Dame, tearing down the gallery of kings and removing all valuables. It was also used to store food.

1804
Napoleon Bonaparte crowned as emperor of France within Notre Dame.

1845
Architect Eugène Viollet-le-Duc begins major restoration project.

1864
Restoration completed.

1871
The cathedral is set on fire during the Paris Commune.

1909
Joan of Arc declared a saint in a ceremony held in Notre Dame.

1939
The windows are removed to avoid damage by German bombers during World War II.

View of Notre Dame from the River Seine.

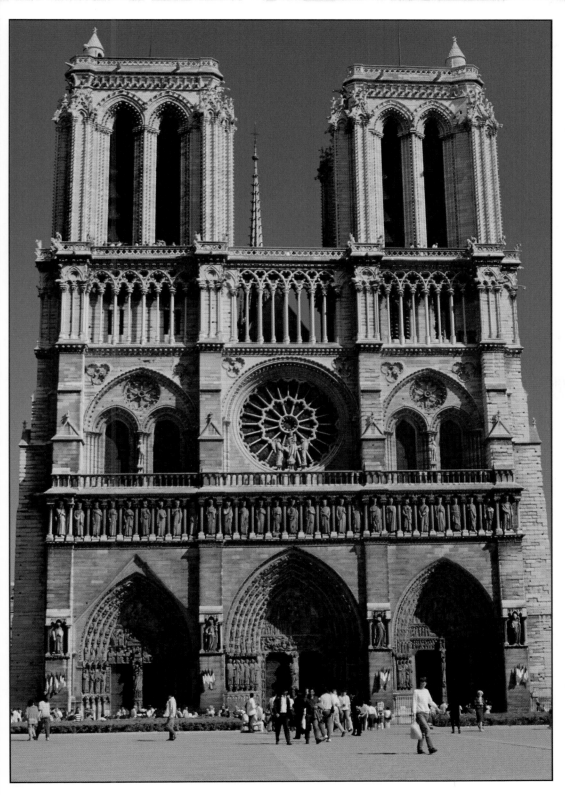

View of the western façade of Notre Dame in Paris.

The *Hunchback of Notre Dame* was originally written in French by Victor Hugo. Notre Dame is the name of the cathedral that stands by the River Seine in the center of the French capital. The novel was published in 1831 under the French title *Notre Dame de Paris*. This translates into English as "Our Lady of Paris," however over the years the novel has come to be known in English as *The Hunchback of Notre Dame*. This is slightly misleading though, as Quasimodo, the hunchback, is not particularly the main character. Several other characters are developed just as well, such as the evil archdeacon Claude Frollo and the tragic heroine, Esmeralda. Many readers would argue that the main character is the cathedral itself.

Poster advertising the 1939 film of The Hunchback of Notre Dame *starring Charles Laughton and Maureen O'Hara.*

The novel was published in 1831 and was very popular. In fact, it was influential in saving the cathedral itself from destruction. Many old buildings in Paris were being destroyed at the time. The novel was partly responsible for preserving the spectacular Gothic architecture of Notre Dame.

There have been many adaptations of the novel for the big screen, starring some of the world's most famous actors. A few are listed below. These versions have tended to simplify the theme and concerns. Often the focus of these films is the mistreatment of

Quasimodo for his ugliness, the moral being that one should not judge people by their looks, however this is a very small part of Victor Hugo's original novel.

- *The Hunchback of Notre Dame* (1923), silent film starring Lon Chaney as Quasimodo
- *The Hunchback of Notre Dame* (1939), starring Charles Laughton with Maureen O'Hara as Esmeralda
- *The Hunchback of Notre Dame* (1956), starring Anthony Quinn with Gina Lollobrigida as Esmeralda
- *The Hunchback of Notre Dame* (1982), a TV movie starring Anthony Hopkins as Quasimodo and Derek Jacobi as Frollo
- *The Hunchback of Notre Dame* (1996), animated film by Walt Disney Pictures, featuring talking gargoyles named Victor and Hugo and having a happy ending

Early Medieval Paris

From about 1000 AD, Paris was ruled by the Capetian family. At first they controlled little more than Paris, but over the centuries their wealth and power grew. Paris also grew in importance as a royal capital and as a center for both learning and the Catholic Church.

By the 12th century, the city already had distinct districts. The Île de la Cité, on which Notre Dame was built in 1163, was the center of government and religious life. The Left Bank was the center of learning. The Right Bank was the financial district – a league of merchants quickly became a powerful force in the city's affairs.

In 1180, King Philippe Auguste started a number of major building works in the city. He built a new city wall and began the construction of the Louvre Palace. His grandson Louis IX, who was renowned for his extreme holiness (and later canonized as St. Louis), made the city a major center of pilgrimage in the 13th century. He completed the construction of Notre Dame, Sainte-Chapelle on the Île de la Cité, and also the Saint Denis Basilica.

The Capetian line died out in 1328, leaving no male heir. Edward III of England claimed the French throne because he was the grandson of Philip IV of France. However his claim was rejected by the French barons, who supported the claim of Philippe of Valois. This argument led to The Hundred Years War between France and England.

After the revolt, King Charles V of France built a new city wall to protect against invaders, while inside the city the Bastille was built. This was a prison to control the restless population. Another revolt, this time over taxation, broke out in 1382, but it was quickly and violently suppressed.

Civil war broke out in France after the assassination of Louis of Valois. In the chaos that followed, the English led by Henry V captured Paris in 1420. After Henry's death, Charles VII of France tried but failed to retake the city in 1429, despite the assistance of Joan of Arc (who was wounded in the attempt). The following year, Henry VI of England was crowned King of France at Notre Dame at age 10. In 1437, Charles finally managed to retake the city after several failed sieges.

Over the following years, Valois kings of France and the nobility built several impressive churches and mansions in Paris. In the century that followed, the city's population more than tripled.

DURING THE LIFETIME OF VICTOR HUGO

1802
February 26th – Victor Hugo is born in Besançon, France.

1815
June 18th – England defeats France at Battle of Waterloo, Napoleon's last battle.

1815 – 1818
Hugo attends the Lycée Louis-Le Grand in Paris.

1821
Hugo's mother dies.

1822
Hugo wins a pension of 1,000 francs a year from King Louis XVIII.
Marries Adéle Foucher.

1823
Hugo's first novel, *Han d'Islande* (Han of Iceland) is published.

1831
Hugo's *The Hunchback of Notre Dame* is published.

1833
Actress Juliette Drouet became his mistress and, supported by a small pension, she became his unpaid secretary and travelling companion for the next fifty years.

1843
Hugo's daughter Léopoldine drowns.

1845
Hugo is made a peer of France by King Louis Philippe.

1848
All French men now given the chance to vote. Women are not given the same rights for almost another century.

1850
King Louis Philippe dies.

1851
After the unsuccessful revolt against President Louis Napoleon (later Emperor Napoleon III), Hugo flees to Brussels.

1852
Hugo moves to Jersey.

1853
Hugo's best known works of poetry, *Les Chatiments* (Punishments), is published.

1855
Hugo moves to Guernsey.

1862
Les Misérables, Hugo's longest and most famous work, is published.

1868
Hugo's wife, Adèle, dies.

1870
Hugo makes a triumphant return to Paris and is elected to the National Assembly.

1876
Hugo is elected to the Senate.

1878
Hugo suffers a mild stroke.

1883
Hugo's mistress, Juliette Drouet, dies.

1885
May 22nd – At the age of eighty-three, Victor Hugo dies from a stroke in Paris.
June 1st – Millions of people line the streets of Paris as Victor Hugo's funeral procession carries him for burial in the Panthéon in Paris.

The Panthéon in Paris.

The coronation of Napoleon Bonaparte (1769–1821), Emperor of France, and of Empress Josephine, at Notre Dame Cathedral, Paris, December 2, 1804.

Other Works Written By VICTOR HUGO

NOVELS
1823 – Han of Iceland
1826 – Bug-Jargal
1829 – The Last Days of a Condemned Man
1831 – The Hunchback of Notre Dame
1834 – Claude Gueux
1862 – Les Misérables
1866 – Toilers of the Sea
1869 – The Man Who Laughs
1873 – Ninety-Three

PLAYS
1827 – Cromwell
1829 – Marion de Lorme
1830 – Hernani
1832 – The King Takes His Amusement
1833 – Lucrèce Borgia
1833 – Marie Tudor
1835 – Angelo
1838 – Ruy Blas
1843 – The Burgraves
1882 – Torquemada

Victor Hugo also wrote hundreds of poems, speeches, historical and literary essays, and newspaper articles.

INDEX

FURTHER INFORMATION

IF YOU LIKED THIS BOOK, YOU MIGHT ALSO WANT TO TRY THESE TITLES IN THE BARRON'S *GRAPHIC CLASSICS* SERIES:

Journey to the Center of the Earth
Kidnapped
Moby Dick
Oliver Twist
Treasure Island

FOR MORE INFORMATION ON VICTOR HUGO:

www.hugo-online.org

www.victorhugo.gg